Charlie the Champ

For every clever little monkey!

Based on original illustrations by Jo Ryan

This book was made by Mara van der Meer,
Penny Worms and Kate Ward.

Copyright © 2017 St. Martin's Press

Published by priddy books
53–64 Chancery Lane, London, WC2A 1QT

3 5 7 9 10 8 6 4 2

Manufactured in China

Images credited to iStock Photo: Whistle © Sashkinw; Elephant dung © yogesh_more; Fan © ryasick;
Stripy headband © t_kimura; Red headband © Mark Herreid; Pom-poms © IG_Royal; Blue flag © Memitina;
Rubber ring © offstocker; Diving mask © abadonian; Lily pads © cyoginan; Lightbulb © kyoshino.
Images credited to Alamy: Pink feather boa © Superstock / Alamy. All other images © St. Martin's Press.

Charlie the Champ

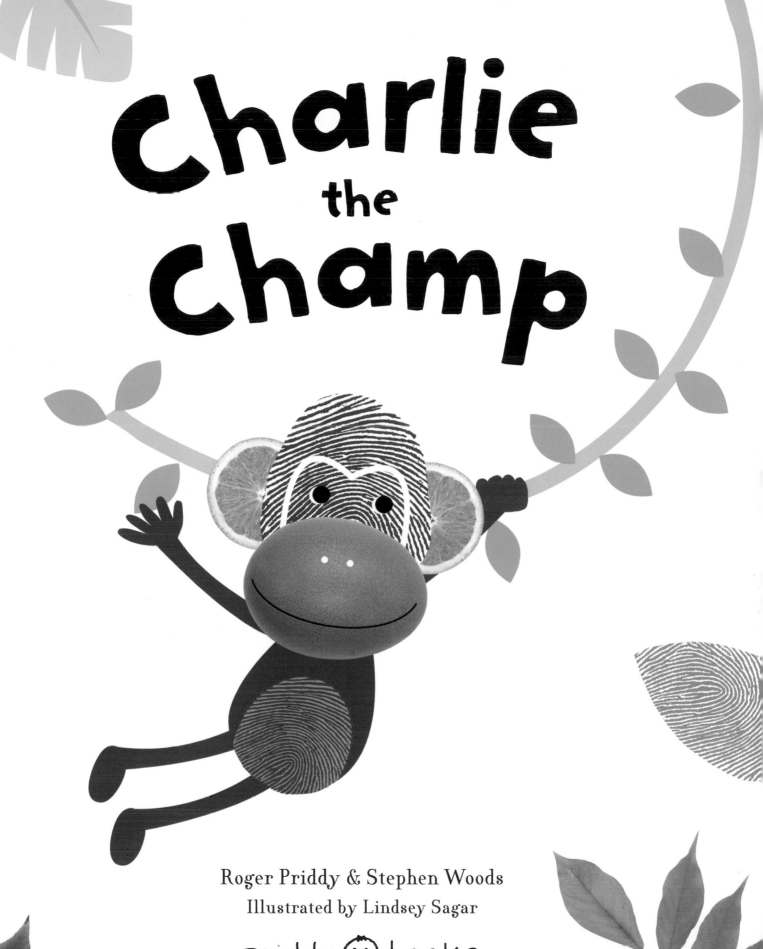

Roger Priddy & Stephen Woods
Illustrated by Lindsey Sagar

priddy books

I'm the fastest.

To the east of the Limpopo,
by some cool freshwater springs,
the animals were arguing
over who was best at things.

Let's have a competition then, a sort of Jungle Games.

"Good idea!" they all agreed.
"A chance to prove our claims!"

But Charlie Chimp, she felt so sad.
She'd never won a prize.
She wished there was a competition
just for being wise.

Just do your best, Charlie.

The games began with racing
down the narrow, dusty track.
The whistle blew and off they ran,
leaving Charlie at the back!

But looking up, she saw her chance,
as Lion won the race.
She grabbed a vine and flew
right through the air to second place!

"First to cross the river"
was the next trial of the day.
But little Charlie worried
that she might get swept away.

The whistle blew and Crocodile sped off –
he couldn't fail!
But clever Charlie grabbed a ride
by clinging to his tail!

Hide-and-seek was next –
to find a place that they could squeeze.
Poor Hippo's big, round bottom
wouldn't fit behind the trees!

Charlie thought she'd won this time.
She curled up in a ball.

But Chameleon turned the colour of a tree
and fooled them all.

For the final test, the tug of war,
Team Rhino took the strain.
The others huffed and puffed,
but it was hopelessly in vain.

So little Charlie, thinking fast,
just pulled a funny face.

She made them laugh, and put them off.
Team Charlie got first place!

And later, at a party
lit with stars and fireflies,
they cheered as little Charlie
won the "Cheeky Monkey" prize!